Indian Shoes

Also by Cynthia Leitich Smith

JINGLE DANCER

RAIN IS NOT MY INDIAN NAME

Indian Shoes

CYNTHIA LEITICH SMITH

Illustrated by Jim Madsen

HARPERCOLLINSPUBLISHERS

Library of Congress Cataloging-in-Publication Data

Smith, Cynthia Leitich.

Indian shoes / Cynthia Leitich Smith ; illustrated by Jim Madsen.

p.   cm.

Summary: Together with Grampa, Ray Halfmoon, a Seminole-Cherokee
boy, finds creative and amusing solutions to life's challenges.

ISBN 0-06-029531-7 — ISBN 0-06-029532-5 (lib. bdg.)

[1. Grandfathers—Fiction.   2. Indians of North America—Fiction.]   I.
Madsen, Jim, date, ill.   II. Title.

PZ7.S6446 In   2002   2001039510

[Fic]—dc21   CIP

                                                                      AC

Typography by Karin Paprocki

12 13 SCP 20 19 18 17 16 15 14 13 12 11

First Edition

For my grandmothers, Dorothy and Melba,
in memory of my grandfathers,
Clifford and Ray,
and in memory of my stepgrandpa, Herb

With thanks to: Anne Bustard;
Toni Buzzeo; Frances Hill, who suggested collage;
my aunt Gail McCauley, for telling me about
the barbershop; my very cute husband, Greg;
my agent, Ginger Knowlton;
the HarperCollins Children's Books marketing
team; Marisa Miller; and especially my editor,
Rosemary Brosnan, who believed that these two
characters belonged in children's literature
and found a place for them

Contents

Indian Shoes

Indian Shoes

Ray and Grampa Halfmoon traipsed down the cracked sidewalk of a steel and stone city. Ray tracked Grampa's steps, danced to the *rat-a-tat-a-clang* of a trash-can band, and skipped beneath the ruffling branches.

"Let's duck in here," Grampa Halfmoon began, "and say 'Morning.'"

When the wind whistled into Murphy Family Antiques, Ray and Grampa whistled in with it. At the welcome mat, Grampa said "Morning" to Junior Murphy. Ray retied his neon orange shoelaces and took a look around the store.

The shop <u>brimmed</u> with treasures: an autographed baseball . . . a Chinese lantern . . . ostrich feathers . . . a basket of antique buttons on a pedestal . . . a tabletop held up by a real elephant leg . . . a moose head mounted high on a wall.

Where are the coats that matched the old buttons? Ray wondered. What happened to the rest of the elephant? Who took the body of the moose glaring down?

Grampa asked, "Do you see that?"

A pair of men's moccasins waited in a glass box on a pedestal. The card read:

SEMINOLE MOCCASINS
FROM OKLAHOMA
$150 $100 $75 $50 OR
BEST OFFER

Grampa Halfmoon told Ray, "These put me in the mind of bein' back home."

For a long moment, they both looked at the moccasins. But Ray's mind was mostly on their afternoon plans, and his gaze wandered to the autographed baseball.

"We'd best get a move on," Grampa said, "to today's Cubs game."

Grampa and Ray left the shop with matching grins. They rode the rattling elevated train to Wrigley Field and watched the Cubs take on the St. Louis Cardinals.

From the first inning on, Grampa Halfmoon told old-time Cherokee, Seminole, and family stories. "Every once in a great while, my gramps used to wear moccasins," Grampa said, "instead of his cowboy boots." Grampa paused a moment to study the Cubs' scoreboard. "He used to pitch to me and my cousins, too, and Gramps usually struck us out. Then he'd jump in the lake to cool down afterward, just like us kids. The lakes back home in Oklahoma . . . those are the prettiest lakes I've ever seen."

Ray frowned, thinking it over. Not far away, Lake Michigan lapped against the shores of Chicago, a fierce blue blanket alongside the park. It was a pretty lake, Ray decided. A lot bigger than the lakes in Oklahoma. More sailboats.

After the seventh-inning stretch, Ray and

Grampa Halfmoon ordered hot dogs.

"Now, these Chicago hot dogs," Grampa said, "they're dandy, but every now and then I get a hankering for some of that crackle-fried bacon your Aunt Wilhelmina likes to make. You know, that woman fries everything she cooks. I saw her fry a whole turkey once for Christmas, and it was sure enough some big bird."

Ray bit into his hot dog. He knew all about Aunt Wilhelmina's cooking. Ray and Grampa drove their pickup down to visit her and Uncle Leonard in Oklahoma once or twice a year. What he didn't know was why Grampa Halfmoon was thinking so hard today about Aunt Wilhelmina's crackle-fried bacon.

When the wind carried a home-run baseball into the stands, Ray almost caught it.

Cheers filled the air, but Grampa Halfmoon didn't make much of a fuss.

He was homesick, Ray realized.

Ray wiggled his toes inside the hightops

with the neon orange shoelaces. He couldn't afford a bus ticket to Oklahoma, but he had an idea. Ray thought about it during the last two innings of the game and while riding on the rattling elevated train all the way back to the stop nearest his redbrick <u>bungalow</u>.

Meanwhile Grampa Halfmoon talked about this wild-haired mutt he'd had when he was a kid and how he'd named it Catastrophe. Grampa talked about Ray's parents, who were killed by a tornado back when Ray was just a babe. And Grampa talked about how he used to take Ray's daddy fishing by starlight.

At bedtime the wind breathed against the stained-glass pane in Ray's bedroom window. He dumped jangling money—twenty-eight dollars and sixty-seven cents—out of his jar and onto his woolly blanket.

It was the most money Ray had ever owned at one time, but it wasn't enough.

Or was it? The sign had said "$50 or Best Offer." Maybe the best offer would be a little less than thirty bucks. Maybe the best offer would come from Ray.

On Monday after school, Ray marched down the cracked sidewalk. He held tight to his money jar, danced to the *rat-a-tat-a-clang* of a trash-can band, and skipped beneath the ruffling branches.

When the wind blew into Murphy Family Antiques again, Ray blew in again with it. At the welcome mat, he retied his neon orange shoelaces and said "Afternoon" to Junior Murphy. Then Ray breezed by the table with the elephant leg and the basket full of antique buttons. He paused behind a lady who was carrying a library book.

The lady seemed interested in the moccasins. "Do you know if these are real?" she asked. "Native American worn and Native American made?"

"I could double-check," Junior Murphy answered, "but it might take a while."

"I don't have a while to wait," the lady replied. "And I don't walk by this way too often." She hugged the library book a little tighter. "I'll tell you what. I could give you thirty dollars for them now, but that's all my budget will allow."

Ray shook his head at the moose. Thirty dollars topped his best bid.

Just then the wind rushed in. The door sounded *ka-bam*! Ostrich feathers fluttered. A Chinese lantern whirled to catch on the moose's antlers. The autographed baseball splashed into the button basket, toppling the pedestal. Buttons whizzed everywhere!

Ray thought, This is my last chance. "I'll give twenty-eight dollars and sixty-seven cents for the moccasins," he told Junior Murphy, "and I'll pick up every last button, too."

"Sorry, Ray," Junior said. "This shop needs the money more than I need the time."

The lady looked at Ray like she wanted to say something, but then she set her book on the counter and wrote a check to pay for the moccasins.

The wind died silent, and Ray felt like the

elephant that had lost a leg to the tabletop. He rocked in his hightops with the orange shoelaces. He stared at the autographed baseball in the mess of buttons. He thought about the stories Grampa Halfmoon had told at the Cubs game and on the train ride home.

When the lady opened the door to leave, the wind gusted in and shoved her back over the welcome mat. Suddenly Ray knew what to do.

"Wanna trade?" he asked the lady. "I've got some Indian shoes you could use. Beats me who made 'em, but they're for-sure Indian worn."

The lady shifted the book beneath her arm and held tight to her purchase. Ray just knew that he and Grampa Halfmoon had lost out. But then the lady's gaze fell to Ray's feet. She chuckled, and they left the shop together.

When the wind whispered against the brick bungalow that night, Grampa slid his feet into the moccasins. "These really take me back," he said. "They feel like home."

Come Tuesday morning, at the high school four blocks away, the librarian placed a pair of beat-up hightops with neon orange shoelaces in her Native American books display. She propped a laser-printed card to the right of the toes. The card read:

Traded from Ray Halfmoon
Cherokee-Seminole Hightops
Not Indian Made, but Indian Worn
(Guaranteed)

"Don't Forget the Pants!"

As Ray and Grampa Halfmoon climbed a flight of stairs to the front terrace of the rented mansion, Jonah appeared to greet them. "Welcome to the wedding," he said.

"I believe, Ray," Grampa began, smoothing his church tie, "that you and the groom have some business to attend to."

Grampa was right. That afternoon Jonah, a Polish-Menominee from Chicago, was marrying their friend Nancy Lee, a Choctaw girl who'd moved to town from Norman, Oklahoma. She'd been friends with the

Halfmoons for only a year or s
that every kid in the bride's
families was a girl, Ray had agreed to p
in as their ring bearer.

Ray had never been to a wedding before.
He knew he'd have to carry the ring down an
aisle in front of a lot of staring people and,
worse, a video camera. Ray's stomach flopped
and flipped just thinking about it, but he was
looking forward to the wedding cake.

Jonah bent down in his gray tux. "This
was my grandmother's wedding ring," he
explained, digging it out of his breast pocket.
"Today it'll become Nancy Lee's."

Ray watched as Jonah set the white gold
band in his palm. Tiny diamonds glittered.
The metal felt cool in Ray's hand.

"Sure is pretty," said Grampa, who was
carrying Ray's belt, socks, and dress shoes.

"I'll take good care of it," Ray said, curling
his fingers tight. He looked down at his fist
and then handed the ring to Grampa. "I
mean, *we'll* take good care of it."

Jonah grinned, all bright blue eyes and dimples. "I'd appreciate that," Jonah said. "As it turns out, Nancy Lee remembered everything except a pillow to carry it on."

Ray couldn't understand why he'd need a pillow to carry the ring. He'd been carrying things his whole life without a pillow.

"That's how it goes with weddings," Grampa said, slipping the ring into his jacket

pocket. "This or that always goes wrong."

Ray and Grampa Halfmoon walked past a window framed in forest green velvet curtains, climbed a spiral staircase, strolled down a hallway with fuzzy burgundy wallpaper, and joined the groomsmen in an upstairs bedroom. A row of rented gray tuxes and crisp, white shirts had been hung in the closet, and Grampa pulled out the smallest sizes in each after handing Ray his belt, socks, and dress shoes.

"This'll look mighty handsome on you," Grampa said, leaving on the plastic wrap.

Ray headed toward the bathroom to get dressed for the wedding.

"Need any help?" Grampa called, shaking hands with the best man.

"Nope," Ray said, "I'll be okay." He'd already tried on the tux at the fitting, and Ray figured once he'd dressed, he could always ask for Grampa's expertise with the tie. He didn't want to look like a little kid in front of the groomsmen.

When Ray shut the heavy door behind him, he was happy to find a full-length mirror on the back of it. In no time, he'd pulled off his Cubs T-shirt and neon purple sweatpants. He'd hooked the two hangers over the crystal doorknob and torn away the plastic covering his crisp, white shirt.

Before long he had it on and buttoned straight. Ray thought he looked just fine in the shirt and his two-day-old trim from Bud's Barbershop.

Feeling braver, he decided to take on the bow tie. The bow itself was already tied, and there was a little hook and a little loophole for fastening around the collar.

Aha! Ray thought. I can do this. I won't even need Grampa's help.

Seconds later Ray studied his reflection in the mirror, wearing the bow tie just right. Now it was time for the jacket and slacks.

But when he slipped the gray jacket off the hanger, its matching pants were nowhere to be found. The second hanger was empty. Ray quickly pulled on the jacket, opened the bathroom door a crack, and called for Grampa Halfmoon.

"How're you doin' in there?" Grampa asked, walking over with a white rosebud boutonniere.

Ray stepped back from the door to let him in. "No pants," he said, holding up the empty hangers. "Can you double-check in the closet?"

Grampa set the boutonniere on the counter and sped off, while Ray waited in the bathroom. A couple of minutes later, Grampa returned and shut the bathroom door.

"No pants," Grampa Halfmoon confirmed. "I checked three times."

They could still hear the groomsmen laughing outside about who-knew-what, but in the bathroom, nothing seemed too funny.

Ray shifted his weight from one sock-clad foot to another. "I can't go out there in my underwear," he said, holding up his neon purple sweatpants. "Can I just wear these?"

"I don't reckon so," Grampa answered. "Everybody'd be starin' at you instead of Nancy Lee."

Rap-rap-rap-rap came a knock on the bathroom door. Ray and Grampa heard the best man's friendly voice. "Ten minutes until show time," he said.

"Can't we just get another pair of pants?" Ray asked.

Grampa shook his head. "Not in ten minutes. But I have another idea."

Grampa excused himself to see if any of the guests were sporting pants Ray's size. Meanwhile Ray paced and puttered and made faces at himself in the mirror.

Six minutes later, Grampa Halfmoon returned empty-handed. The only other kids at the wedding were frilly girls, he reported. The kind with lace and bows.

"Too bad I can't borrow your pants," Ray said. "But I'd drown in them."

For another minute, Ray and Grampa tried to come up with a solution. They even thought about Grampa pitching in for Ray, becoming the oldest ring bearer ever, but they decided he couldn't do that without being specially asked.

Then Grampa Halfmoon stepped out to talk to the best man about handling the ring delivery, but he'd already left with the groomsmen to usher. So Grampa searched for someone else. But the groom was talking to his daddy in one room, and the bride was hugging her auntie in the other.

"No luck," Grampa announced, returning to Ray. He glanced at his pocket watch. "We've got about a minute and a half."

Ray felt like his bow tie was strangling him. "I can't go out there half naked," he replied.

Grampa looked from his own pants to Ray's bare legs. "Maybe you can borrow my slacks after all. At least it's worth a try."

At the last *rap-rap-rap-rap* knock, Ray stared at his reflection. He looked smart enough in the white shirt, tux jacket, white rosebud boutonniere, and Grampa's church slacks, rolled at the waist and leg bottoms, held tight by his own leather belt.

He grinned at Grampa, standing there in his boxer shorts, and said, "It'll do."

"You look like your daddy did back when he got married," Grampa said. "Except shorter, don't you know?"

As a harp began to sing, Ray marched out of the bathroom, through the hallway with the fuzzy burgundy wallpaper, down the spiral staircase, and past a window framed in forest green velvet curtains, barely in time to start down the aisle.

The maid of honor led him in front of the line of bridesmaids to a little girl, no older than five. She gripped a basket of white rose petals and stared at him with scared, watery eyes. Ray couldn't help feeling sorry for her. He was pretty nervous himself.

"Don't worry," he said. "We'll do all right."

After all, Ray thought, the worst part is behind me.

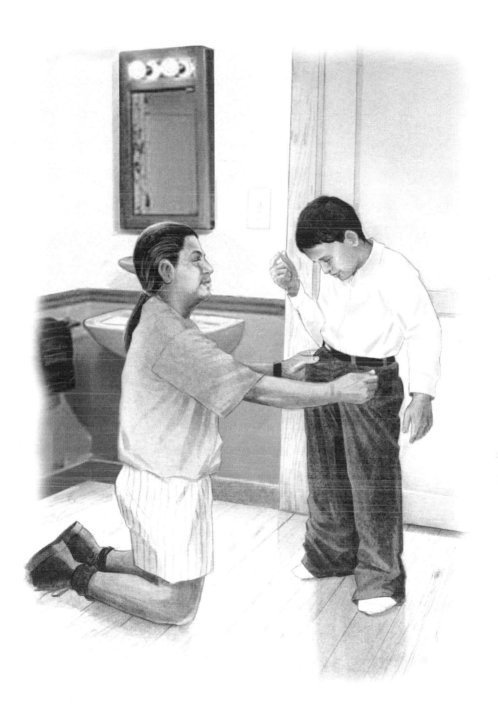

Just then, Ray realized he'd forgotten the wedding ring.

Grampa Halfmoon still had it upstairs in his jacket pocket.

Uh-oh, Ray thought. I'll never make it back in time.

Racing around bridesmaids, he was just about to shoot up the spiral stairs when he spotted Grampa Halfmoon peeking from behind one of the forest green velvet curtains. A lace-trimmed tablecloth had been tied around his waist. In his outstretched hand, waiting for Ray, was Nancy Lee's diamond ring.

Guess Who's Coming to Dinner?

A cut pine glowed in crimson bubble lights. Flames danced in the fireplace. A newly arrived card from Jonah and Nancy Lee stood among those gathered on the mantle. Frosty webs clung to windowpanes, and the wind groaned against the rooftop.

This was the first Christmas Day that Ray and Grampa Halfmoon hadn't celebrated with family in Oklahoma, but last week the pickup had quit for good. Just as well, Grampa had said, what with the roads so slick. While riding the rattling train home from church, Ray had promised himself to act merry anyway, for Grampa's sake.

Snow swirled around Ray and Grampa Halfmoon as they waded through the drifts, beneath the ice-sculpted maples to the Murphy home. Glittering snowflakes smacked wet against Ray's cheeks and clouded the mourning midday sky.

In the Murphy family kitchenette, Ray said "Merry Christmas" to Prince, who yipped and tripped over his paws and slipped on the linoleum. Ray searched for the biscuit box while Grampa escorted Prince onto the back step to do his business.

When it was time to leave, Ray rubbed Prince's belly and said, "It's tough being alone on holidays."

Ray's and Grampa's breath puffed cloudy as they trudged next door to the Wang home. In the driveway, Mrs. Wang's VW Bug waited to be freed from the snow like a triceratops skeleton embedded in rock.

Inside Mrs. Wang's home office, Grampa said "Good tidings" to Tank, who snoozed in his shell, and to Eugenia the parrot, who replied, *"Feliz Navidad."* While Grampa spied on Tank, Ray refilled Eugenia's seed mix and offered her a farewell cookie.

"Poor Eugenia," Grampa said, tugging his forest green knit cap over his ears. "Tank's lousy company this time of year."

"'Bye, Eugenia," Ray said, pulling on his wool-lined mittens.

"Joyeux Noel!" Eugenia chirped.

Ray and Grampa tromped two doors down to the Onsi home. Sleet caught in Grampa's shoulder-length ponytail, and Ray's teeth clattered like old bones.

In the Onsis' living room, Ray wrinkled his nose and said "Happy Holidays" to Mama Ferret and her kittens, who slinked below the plush, L-shaped pit sofa.

"Kinda smelly, aren't they?" Ray asked, unwrapping his scarf.

"Yep," Grampa Halfmoon replied.

Ray cleaned the litter boxes and refilled the food and water bowls. Meanwhile Grampa flicked the feather toy until the ferret family emerged to tumble and play tag. But one kit wouldn't have any of that.

The runt raced back and forth with chow in his teeth, snatching it from a bowl and hiding it beneath the sofa.

"Poor Mama," Grampa Halfmoon said. "She sure has her paws full."

Ray and Grampa slid through the slush across the street to the Wilson home. Layers of cotton and flannel and denim and down weren't enough to still their shivers or keep the goose bumps from rising on their skin.

Inside Mr. Wilson's studio, Grampa said "Season's Greetings" to Legs, who blinked at him with eight eyes. Ray gave her crickets to munch while Grampa served up a juicy earthworm. Legs gnawed the squirmy worm first.

"I'm partial to Legs," Grampa Halfmoon said. "She has a beautiful soul."

The sky deepened to murky twilight as Ray and Grampa shuffled back to their brick bungalow. Ray's lungs ached from the frigid air, and the wind whooshed away the crunchy boot prints he and Grampa left behind them.

In front of their toasty fire, Ray sipped steaming cocoa while Grampa sank into his worn recliner and clicked on the evening news. Ray watched stories about Santa, soup kitchens, and ice skaters on State Street. From O'Hare Airport to Lake Shore Drive, the storm blanketed Ray's steel and stone city in glistening white. Entire blocks had lost power, and repairs lagged hours, even days, behind.

"Check on your neighbors," the reporter warned. "Cold can become deadly fast."

Though memories of Aunt Wilhelmina's pecan pie, Uncle Leonard's hearty chuckle, and the Elvis Christmas CD haunted Ray, at least he had the glow of the crimson bubble lights, the steam of the cocoa, turkey roasting in the kitchen, and Grampa for company.

Could be a lot worse, Ray thought.

Just as he swallowed his last sip of cocoa, the TV screen and ceiling-fan bulb flickered off. The bubble lights died, dulling the pine tree, and the gurgling heater fell silent.

Grampa climbed out of his recliner, strode

to the window, and peered outside. "Street-light's out," he said. "I'm guessing the whole block at least."

"The pets!" Ray exclaimed, moving to his side. "What about the pets?"

Grampa Halfmoon slung an arm around Ray's shoulders. "We can't very well build a fire at every home on the block, but . . . Let's see how we're farin' first."

Ray trudged after Grampa into the shadowy, cramped kitchen and watched him take a pan of half-cooked turkey legs out of the oven. The plastic packages of frozen okra and rice pilaf were still ice blocks in the freezer. The brownies were still powder in a box.

No road trip, no Aunt Wilhelmina or Uncle Leonard, and now no holiday meal. It was the worst Christmas ever, but all Ray could think about was Prince, Tank, Eugenia, Mama Ferret, her kits, and Legs.

"Too bad their families left them all alone," Ray grumbled, setting his empty mug next to the sink. "Too bad the pets can't just come over here."

Right then Grampa Halfmoon's eyes crinkled, and Ray grinned for the first time all day. "Why not?" they asked together.

It took Ray's wooden sled, Grampa's squeaky wheelbarrow, two oversized beach towels, and a couple of the pets' own zip-up carriers. It took some ruffled fur and feathers and leg hair and nerves. It took more than an

hour of wading through the drifts, beneath branches draped by icicles, and listening to Eugenia chirp *"Mele Kalikimaka!"* which meant Merry Christmas in Hawaiian.

But finally . . . Tank the turtle, hibernating in his aquarium . . . Eugenia the parrot, chatting on her swing . . . Mama Ferret and her kittens, tumbling in their cage . . . and Legs the tarantula, sauntering in his giant plastic skull . . . had settled in the Halfmoon family room. Prince, the fox-faced Pomeranian, curled on the matted shag carpet in front of the fireplace.

To Ray and Grampa Halfmoon, the giant marshmallows, scavenged from the cabinet, roasted over the flames, tasted charred and chewy and sweet.

And even though the blizzard was blustering, the bubble lights had died, the turkey legs were ruined, the pickup had puttered out, the road trip was canceled, and the rest of their family had gathered miles away, Christmas suddenly seemed like Christmas.

Ray laughed at the frolicking ferrets. "Like rats but funny," he said.

"More like polecats," Grampa said, downing a marshmallow. "How 'bout you pick out a kit? I told the Onsis we'd take one of those smelly ferrets, if that suits you."

It did. Ray noticed the ferret runt eyeing his marshmallow. From now on, Ray planned to keep watch for swiped treasures beneath the couch. "I'm gonna call him Bandit," he announced. "Thanks, Grampa."

"Merry Christmas," Grampa Halfmoon replied.

And then Eugenia squawked, "Happy New Year!"

The Accident

Grampa Halfmoon's hand felt sure on Ray's shoulder, guiding him down the cracked sidewalk from school toward their redbrick bungalow. That afternoon the bus stop looked run down, the trash-can band banged *rat-a-rat-a-ka-plop*, and Annie's Children's Bookstore was closed for remodeling. But Ray didn't mind. He was too excited.

"It's an art contest," he told Grampa. "For all the kids in the city. The three big winners' pictures are gonna be hung up in the window of a store on State Street."

Grampa grinned. "I guess that means you'll be enterin'."

"Maybe I'll win a blue ribbon," Ray said. "We could take the El train to see my picture and . . . maybe grab some hot dogs."

"Your mama loved to paint," Grampa said. "She'd paint the side of a barn or a barn on a canvas." Then he promised Ray that they'd get some hot dogs, win or lose.

Ray held out his hand to seal the deal, and Grampa shook it.

After finishing up his math homework, Ray decided it was time to paint.

Bandit the ferret perched on Ray's shoulder, watching him dip the paintbrush in a Dixie cup of clear water. Ray had placed one of Grampa Halfmoon's moccasins on the bookshelf beside his antique desk. He stared at it a few minutes and then moved the brush wand to cover the bristles with brown paint.

Before long Ray had created a blob on his paper.

He squinted at it this way and that, wondering if the blob could pass for a shoe.

Just then Grampa shuffled into the room in his slippers and plaid pajamas. Not noticing his own moccasin, he remarked, "My, that's sure a fine potato."

Ray turned off his brass desk lamp, scrambled under his woolly blanket, and tried not to show his hurt feelings. He knew Grampa would've never said anything to make him feel bad on purpose. Ray just couldn't paint like his mama had.

After Grampa had kissed his forehead and shuffled out, Ray listened to the rain whisper against his stained-glass window.

'S okay, he thought. I've got until Friday.

The next day after supper, Bandit hid a stinky sock behind the bookshelves as Ray sharpened his pencil, set out a cup of water, and placed a fresh sheet of paper on his antique desk.

Searching for inspiration, Ray spotted a book titled *Dinosaur*. He flipped through until finding a photo he liked and then carefully sketched a fierce *T. rex*. It didn't quite look like the skeleton shown in the book, but Ray could tell what it was.

That's no potato, he thought, dipping the bristles of the paintbrush into the water.

Ray's book said that some scientists thought dinosaurs came in bright colors, like the lizards of today. The idea struck Ray as a good one, and he traced the pencil outline in bright orange paint.

Better, Ray thought. I'm getting better at this.

Excited, Ray plopped the brush back in the Dixie cup, turning the water bright orange. Then he rolled the bristles in red paint to fill in the *T. rex*'s form. The second his brush hit the paper, Ray knew he'd made a mistake—too much water.

Red paint puddled in the middle of the dino body, then streamed off in all directions. Using his brush, Ray tried to direct the flow, but it was no use. His fierce *T. rex* had bloomed into a sunny marigold. He studied the flower as it dried.

Problem is, Ray thought, I'm not much of a marigold kind of guy.

On Wednesday night, Ray set up another Dixie cup of water and another fresh sheet of paper. Then he sketched a fiery sun, a towering oak, and a redbrick bungalow with a stained-glass window on one side and smoke coming out of the chimney.

When he dipped his paintbrush into the cup, Ray carefully used just the right amount of water. He cleaned the bristles between colors, stopping to change the water in his cup twice. Finally satisfied, Ray let the masterpiece dry under his brass desk lamp.

Grampa shuffled in, whistling long and low. "You sure outdid yourself there. If those judges don't put a blue ribbon on that one, they don't know nothin'. But you're runnin' late for bedtime. So you get yourself into bed, and I'll be your cleanup crew."

As Grampa tucked Ray beneath his woolly blanket, Bandit climbed up on the antique desk to see the masterpiece for himself. As he scurried toward the lamp, Bandit's tail brushed against the Dixie cup.

It toppled, rolling, spilling, splashing, plummeting off the desk and onto the hardwood floor below.

Murky water flooded Ray's newly finished painting. Colors swirled and darkened. The paper was soaked through. The fiery sun, the redbrick house, and the towering oak tree vanished into a big, wet, splotchy, ugly, brown mess.

"Bandit!" Ray exclaimed as the culprit escaped to the bookshelves.

Grampa Halfmoon took off to the kitchen for paper towels, but Ray just sat up in bed and shook his head. When Grampa got back, Ray said, "Now I'll never win."

"What's that?" Grampa Halfmoon asked, wiping up the water that had spilled onto Ray's desktop.

Ray pulled his blanket up to his chin. "I've got only one day left. I give up."

Ray half expected Grampa Halfmoon to give him a pep talk.

Instead Grampa answered, "Too bad. I sure was lookin' forward to that hot dog, win or lose. But I guess we won't be going downtown at all then."

On Thursday night, Ray carried Bandit into the family room, filled a Dixie cup with water, returned to his own bedroom, and locked the door behind him.

I've come this far, Ray thought. I might as well see it through. He wanted that hot dog, and he didn't want to disappoint Grampa.

As he set the cup down on his antique desk, rain began to whisper against the stained-glass window. The *shhh*ing sound made Ray settle down a bit and rethink how he wanted to go about putting together his contest entry.

He stared at his ruined masterpiece, still sitting in the middle of his desk.

The night before, Grampa just hadn't had the heart to throw it out.

Amid the dried brown puddle, Ray could

see a bit of the gold of the sun, the red of the brick, and the green of the leaves. He set the painting to one side, then got out a fresh piece of paper. He glanced around the room and noticed that Grampa's moccasin was still perched on his bookshelf.

For a long time, his gaze shifted between the blank page and the ruined picture.

Ray thought back to how he'd wanted to do a painting of one of Grampa's moccasins. That way, he figured, it'd kind of be like the picture belonged to both of us.

Then he took a sip of water from his Dixie cup and began digging through his desk drawer for the rounded scissors and a bottle of glue.

I'm not going to show Grampa when I'm done, Ray thought. I'll let it be a surprise.

Two weeks later, Ray and Grampa took the rattling El train to State Street, stopped by a hot dog stand for lunch, and then joined the sidewalk crowd gawking at the city's best kids' art, proudly displayed in a fancy-schmancy department store window.

Ray's entry wasn't a painting. It was a collage.

That last night before the deadline, Ray had turned his ruined painting into something else. He'd used his rounded scissors to cut the painting into geometric shapes. With his pencil, he'd outlined the shape of one of Grampa Halfmoon's moccasins. Then he'd filled in the outline with multicolored shapes to create shadows and textures, to show how warm and strong the moccasin was, how it could make Grampa feel like home. A dab of glue here and there, and suddenly, Ray had created his entry.

But that's not what made Ray smile. It was the way Grampa pointed and yelled to the crowd, "That's my shoe! That's my shoe!"

Everybody in the crowd looked down at

Grampa's boots, and they didn't know what he was yelling about. But Ray did. Even though his ribbon read "third place," he felt like a first-place winner.

Team Colors

When Ray stumbled in for Pop Tarts, Grampa studied his scraggly bangs. "Morning, sleepybones. With that mess of a mop, you'll never be able to see the ball comin'."

Ray's team, the Bobcats, was scheduled to play its arch rival, the Rockets, later that day. The Rockets boasted the league's powerhouse pitcher; and since Ray had enough trouble at bat, he wasn't much looking forward to the game.

"We're due for a trip to Bud's Barbershop,"

Ray agreed, pushing the scraggly hair out of his eyes.

"Overdue," Grampa answered. "Good thing Bud's not fussy about appointments."

Ray and Grampa traipsed down the cracked sidewalk of a steel and stone city. The day was shaping up to be a scorcher, but a friendly breeze blew by. Ray spotted an orange tabby kitten snoozing in the window of Murphy Family Antiques, a fresh coat of paint dressing up the bus stop, and an ice-cream truck playing "Pop Goes the Weasel."

He couldn't wait to see the barber pole, climb into one of the beat-up swiveling chairs, and listen to talk of the Cubs and City Hall. Ray could almost smell Bud's stinky cigars.

"Barbershop's one of the last places a man can go to be a man," Grampa said, just like always.

Ray thought about how Aunt Wilhelmina would say that kind of talk was old-fashioned foolishness, but he kept quiet. He liked being counted in with the men sometimes. Ray liked everything about Bud's Barbershop, even though he and Grampa hadn't moseyed in since the spring thaw.

Grampa Halfmoon and Ray rounded the corner and looked up the street. Their jaws dropped like hooked catfish. The barber pole was gone. The BUD'S BARBERSHOP sign had been replaced with one that said COIFFURES BY CLAUDIA. And that wasn't the half of it.

When Ray peeked in the window, he saw that the beat-up swiveling chairs had been replaced with shiny mauve ones. The customers in ball caps had been switched for ladies with long, colorful nails. And when a lady with foo-foo hair opened the glass door to leave, Ray couldn't smell the usual stinky cigars. Instead, out came the sweet smell of rose potpourri.

Ray didn't even think about walking into Claudia's, and neither did Grampa.

Ray glanced at his watch. It was already noon, and they had to leave for the game at

2:30. "Now what're we going to do?" he asked.

"It's too late to track down another shop," Grampa said. "Most places are booked solid on Saturdays. But don't worry. I've got a plan."

Back at the house, Grampa fetched the scissors and a towel. Ray sat down in a kitchen chair and draped the towel over his shoulders.

"You've heard me tell about my wild-haired mutt, Catastrophe," Grampa Halfmoon said, setting a salad bowl on top of Ray's head. "Every once in a while, I'd trim the hair out of his eyes. Everybody said it looked right professional."

As Grampa cut Ray's hair, the prickly ends tickled his neck. To keep from squirming, Ray studied the baseball schedule held by banana-shaped magnets to the refrigerator. He day-dreamed about facing down the Rockets' pitcher and—*ka-smack*—hitting a home run.

Before long Grampa Halfmoon took off the bowl and studied his handiwork. "Hmm,"

Grampa said. "Looks a mite lopsided to me."

Ray tried not to worry as more hair fluttered onto the hardwood floor. He tried not to worry when Grampa's normally calm face drew into a perplexed frown.

But then, after too long of a quiet, Grampa finally stopped and said, "Don't you fret. We'll fix this."

At that Ray jumped to his feet and scrambled to the bathroom mirror. His hair looked like it had been hit by a runaway Weedwacker. Big chunks lay choppy, like mismatched puzzle pieces. Here and there, a piece stuck straight or sideways in the air.

"What am I going to do?" Ray asked.

"Now I said don't fret," Grampa answered. "Ever heard of a crew cut?"

Ray shook his head.

"It's short-short," he explained, "like I wore in the service. But we'll need an electric shaver to do it up right."

Ray didn't know what to think about crew cuts, but he was ready to try anything. He listened in as Grampa Halfmoon called a store down the street. Near as Ray could figure, the store was all out of shavers until a new shipment came in next week.

"Well, that's too bad," Grampa was saying. "I guess we'll try something else."

One errand later, Ray sat back on the kitchen chair for a couple of washes, applications, rinses, and dries. Finally he scrambled back to the bathroom mirror. Ray squinted at his hair, parted straight down the middle, one side in neon purple and the other side in neon orange.

Team colors, Ray thought.

The idea had sounded a lot better when Ray'd come up with it than it looked in the mirror in front of him.

As Ray hurried to dress for the game, he wondered what Coach Onsi and his teammates would say. Maybe, he thought, I'll just keep my cap on.

Just then Ray heard Coach Onsi's SUV honk from the driveway.

It was time to go.

"Good luck," Grampa said, deciding not to ride along for the first time ever. "I'll take the El and meet you there. I just have one more thing to look after today. You show those Rockets what for, though, you hear."

Ray hoisted himself into the backseat of the coach's SUV, and his heart slid right down to his toenails. After all that had happened, he couldn't believe Grampa wouldn't be there to cheer him on at the big game. But Ray waved good-bye and grinned so Grampa wouldn't know how upset he was.

Ray kept quiet as Dalton Wang and Luis Wilson tumbled into the backseat beside him, and he kept quiet as Coach Onsi drove them all out to the ballpark. He just grumbled under his breath when Luis asked about the suspicious-looking hair showing around the plastic fastener at the back of his cap. Once they reached the ballpark, Ray plopped down on the end of the team bench.

As of the third inning, the Rockets pitcher had thrown his best game all season. Dalton's pop fly was nabbed by the catcher, and everybody else on the Bobcats team—including Ray—had quickly struck out.

The score was 7–0, Rockets.

As the fifth inning drew to a close, sunshine heated the team bench like a toaster oven. Grampa Halfmoon still hadn't shown up. The score was 12–0, Rockets.

The Bobcats team hadn't put a single player on base.

Their fans had pretty much wilted in the stands.

So far Ray had managed to keep his colorful hair hidden. He'd even kept on his cap under his helmet both times up to bat. But finally sweat started trickling into his eyelashes. Everybody'll see my head sooner or later, he decided, peeling off his cap to wipe his face dry and then raising his sports bottle for a drink of lukewarm water.

As Ray lowered the bottle, he realized his

fellow Bobcats were staring at his neon orange and purple hair. At least, Ray thought, nobody's going to notice the haircut.

"Hey, look at that!" Dalton exclaimed. "Your hair is the team colors."

"Ray, you're up," Coach Onsi said. "Let's see what we can do with some team spirit!"

The team cheered as Ray left the dugout, his neon purple-orange hair in full view. As he slipped his batter's helmet on, the Bobcat fans in the stands joined in. They clapped, stomped, and chanted his name: "Ray! Ray! Ray! Ray!"

Ray smiled at the Rockets pitcher, but lifted his chin to say he meant business.

The Rockets pitcher gave him a puzzled look in return.

"Ray!" Luis called from the bench. "Ray! Isn't that your grampa?"

It sure was. As the sixth inning began, Grampa Halfmoon took his usual seat right behind the team bench, removed his baseball cap, and waved it high to show off hair decorated in the same neon purple-orange as Ray's!

"Hey!" Coach Onsi called. "That's what I call a fan."

The Bobcat crowd cheered twice as loudly. The top rows hollered, "Purple!" The bottom rows answered, "Orange!" Grampa Halfmoon kept waving his cap.

The Rockets pitcher got so distracted that he threw high, he threw wide, he threw low, he threw too close.

The umpire called, "That's a walk!"

As the Bobcats roared, Ray dropped his bat, pumped his fist into the air, and started jogging. He waved at Grampa with one hand and pointed to his head with the other. Grampa Halfmoon waved his cap higher and shouted with the other fans. Ray heard him yell "Purple!" Ray heard him yell "Orange!" Then Ray's sole touched first base.

Night Fishing

Brr-rang-a-rang-a-rang-a-lang! The alarm jangled in the darkness, but Ray couldn't jangle his bones for it. Sleep knitted his eyelids, and a Cherokee Seven Clans quilt wrapped him cozy and safe.

A few weeks ago, Ray and Grampa had driven down to Oklahoma in their new pickup. The old country house where they were staying belonged to Uncle Leonard and Aunt Wilhelmina, and it overlooked a shimmering lake.

"You comin', sleepybones?" Grampa

Halfmoon called from the doorway.

"Too tired," Ray mumbled, breathing deeply to the hum of the air conditioner, promising himself tomorrow night would be different.

After Grampa had already gone to the lake and come on back, the smell of bacon finally roused Ray.

"No fish today?" Ray asked, stumbling out of the bedroom.

"Plenty in the lake, sleepybones," Grampa said. He pulled off his lucky hat and sank into a recliner. "But I was after something bigger." Before Ray could ask what he meant, Grampa was snoring like a rusty hymn. *"Zzzzz . . ."*

In the kitchen, Uncle Leonard poured the orange juice while Aunt Wilhelmina crackle fried bacon, hash browns, and onions.

"No fish today," Ray said, setting out the forks and spoons.

Aunt Wilhelmina chuckled. "Maybe

even fish need to sleep sometime."

Since they'd arrived in Oklahoma, Ray had gone fishing with Grampa every afternoon. But then summer started sizzling, and Grampa started heading out long before sunrise. Every night Grampa asked Ray to join him, but Ray couldn't seem to leave his books be to get enough sleep. He just loved to read into the late, late night.

"It's the hat," Uncle Leonard said. "He told you not to wash his lucky hat."

"Drat that hat," Aunt Wilhelmina answered. "It made the whole house smell fishy."

"It's not the hat," Ray told her. "Grampa caught one catfish after you washed it."

In the heavy midday heat, Ray holed up in the shady tree house that Uncle Leonard had built many years before. The lake blue sky stretched to the horizon. The water below glittered beneath the sun. It was quiet, too. No rattling trains or trash-can bands. Ray could hear the squirrels play tag from limb to limb, and he settled in to listen.

After a while, Uncle Leonard climbed up the wooden ladder to bring Ray a thermos of Aunt Wilhelmina's icy homemade lemonade.

"What brings you to my old tree house?" Uncle Leonard wanted to know.

Ray took a sip and explained, "It's easier to think up here, and I'm trying to figure out why Grampa hasn't been catching any fish."

"That's some mystery," Uncle Leonard replied. "Before your grampa left home for the service, he was the best fisherman in all of the county. One year he got his picture on the front page of the *Daily Press,* holding up . . . a giant catfish, I think it was. Bigger than most hound dogs."

That sounded like a mighty big catfish to Ray, but he'd heard fishing stories before.

Later the sinking sun swelled pumpkin orange and sweet violet. Ray found Grampa working in Aunt Wilhelmina's vegetable garden.

"I'm going with you early tomorrow morning," Ray declared. "We'll bring Aunt Wilhelmina and Uncle Leonard home a whole bucket of fish."

"I'd like to see you up at that hour,

sleepybones," Grampa Halfmoon said, plucking a plump tomato. "But we're not going just for fish."

"What else are we after?" Ray asked.

"Something bigger" is all Grampa would say.

Ray followed Grampa to the porch, where Uncle Leonard rocked on the creaky swing and read the *Cherokee Advocate* on his laptop computer.

"Any news about something in the lake?" Ray asked. "Maybe a gator?"

"Sorry, Ray," Uncle Leonard replied. "No gators in the headlines today."

Ray tried again. "How about a plesiosaur?"

"Please what?" Aunt Wilhelmina asked, opening the storm door.

"It's like a swimming dinosaur," Ray answered. He'd read that scientists sometimes found animals that were thought to be long extinct. "Are we after one of those?"

Grampa shook his head and grinned.

"Let me guess," Ray said. "Something bigger."

Come bedtime, Ray shut his mystery book and announced, "I'm going fishing later on with Grampa."

"In the middle of the night?" Aunt Wilhelmina asked.

"I finished up my reading early," Ray explained, "so I'll be able to get some sleep before it's time to go."

Aunt Wilhelmina took the reading flashlight Ray had stashed beneath the bed. Then she kissed his forehead and said, "I'm just doing my part to help out."

Brr-rang-a-rang-a-rang-a-lang! The alarm jangled in the darkness, but Ray couldn't jangle his bones for it. Sleep knitted his eyelids, and a Cherokee Seven Clans quilt wrapped him cozy and safe.

"You comin', sleepybones?" Grampa Halfmoon called from the doorway.

"Too tired," Ray mumbled, breathing

deeply to the hum of the air conditioner, promising himself tomorrow night would be different.

Then the alarm jangled again. *Brrr-rang-a-rang-a-rang-a-lang!* And Ray's sleepy bones tossed on a pair of cutoffs and a powwow T-shirt. Curiosity had won out.

Long before sunrise, Grampa and Ray sat side by side on the dock. Grampa Halfmoon wore his lucky hat. Ray lifted his lantern and peered out onto the lapping lake. He didn't see anything unusual.

After a while, Grampa handed Ray a fishing rod and cast his own line into the water. The shadow of a hawk crossed the moon, and Ray wondered what it might be like to sail the skies. He still didn't see anything strange or different or even especially big unless he counted the lake itself or the distant, shadowy tree line.

Poip! Down went the float into the lake water, and *ka-splash,* up came a bass, tugging at the line. Grampa knew how to play 'im, though, and that bass landed soon enough in the bucket. Ray couldn't wait to tell Uncle Leonard.

Grampa was fishing like he was the best in the county again.

"That's some fish," Ray said.

"Sure is," Grampa Halfmoon replied, patting Ray on the shoulder.

Moon slipped away. Water splashed the dock. Ducks drifted by.

Suddenly a fireball zoomed across the heavens, leaving a dusty, glowing trail.

"A shooting star!" Ray exclaimed, jumping to his bare feet, wondering if that had been what Grampa was talking about.

But the streak looked no bigger than a cruising gator, a quacking duck, or even an ornery ole bass. Something didn't quite add up.

Just then a glittering quilt of stars rained across the sky's inky blueness, high above

Grampa Halfmoon and Ray. A mirroring array of lights reflected off the lake's shiny blackness, lapping gently below the dock.

"Cool," Ray whispered.

Grampa grinned and rocked back on his boot heels. "I used to take your daddy fishing like this," he said. "Back when he was your age. I can still feel 'im here, now and again."

Ray stood by Grampa, breathing in the lake air, warmed by the wind. He glanced from the glittering lights in the water to the glittering lights in the heavens.

"So can I," Ray said. "So can I."

At breakfast time, Grampa Halfmoon and Ray headed back into the country house. Grampa pulled off his lucky hat and sank into the recliner. Before long, he was snoring like a rusty hymn. *"Zzzzz . . ."*

Uncle Leonard tossed Ray over one shoulder and hauled him into the kitchen, where the smell of frying bacon filled the air.

"Any fish today?" Aunt Wilhelmina asked.

"Yes, ma'am," Ray said, "but that's not all we caught."

Uncle Leonard sat Ray down. "What else was there?"

"Something bigger" is all that Ray would say.

CYNTHIA LEITICH SMITH

has worked in law, public relations, and journalism. She's a mixed blood, enrolled member of the Muscogee (Creek) Nation. She lives in Austin, Texas, with her husband and two gray tabby cats. Visit her online at www.cynthialeitichsmith.com

Cynthia Smith is the author of RAIN IS NOT MY INDIAN NAME, "a wonderful novel of a present-day teen and her patchwork tribe" (*School Library Journal*), and JINGLE DANCER, a picture book that *Publishers Weekly* calls a "heartening portrait of a harmonious meshing of old and new."